For my Grandmothers, Mothers,
Daughters, Granddaughters and Sisters

Sacred Sex

.....Ancient Teachings for Women

Index

Introduction   7

Her Story   19

Feminine and Male   31

Woman   41

Man   53

Saint and The Whore   59

The Monster   71

Healing the Whore and
the Monster   79

Sacred Temples   85

Ancient Codex   91

Love 117

Sacred Sex 121

Questions from the Sisterhood 153

Conclusion 165

Appendix 169

Introduction

Beautiful Ones

There has been a lot of hesitation in my heart to write this book, for this book will bring many changes in your life as a woman, it will change the perception that you have about yourself, and make you realize that women before you were living in a lie, and what you have learned about women has never been truth.

Sacred sex, ancient teachings for women, is not a sexist book, nor feminist, or new age, but it is a knowledge that has been waiting to be revealed for long time.

This book is for the woman because she is the teacher of love for the man in her life, and it is time to remember, for nothing that you will read here will be completely new for you. The emerging of the feminine has brought a woman the recognition of the sacredness of herself; she is remembering, she is coming back to life.

The women, the teachers of love, must realize their power and use it for enlightenment for all the planet, enlightened women will create a beautiful world of peace.

Sacred sex knowledge will bring chaos in a programmed mind; will make the people uncomfortable because they will need to truly face themselves as they are and to move the relationship to a higher understanding of unity and love.

But any knowledge in the world after the chaos of this understanding will be balanced back into the world, eventually.

Before, it would have taken generations for that balance to happen, but now the planet is moving into the fifth dimension and provoking a quickening in the understanding of all human beings. We are, indeed, in Maya time; the process of the mind to understand and embrace the knowledge has been reduced so human beings are able to unravel their hearts.

We are entering in the space where there is no time, there is no such a thing as process, and then there is no such a thing as separation of any kind, only the experience of the Great Spirit flowing through every single life form. Process created the illusion of separation.

Our ancestors experienced these ways of being when there was no separation inside of them; their hearts were "light as a feather", there were no burdens of any kind,

*no guilt, no shame, no attachments, no
fear., ..There was only unconditional love;
because of an understanding of life,
sacredness was everywhere.*

*We are entering again into that portal;
now is the time when the DNA is quickening
and we remember how to get there and cross
that door of the new beginning; the new land
is there.*

*Preparation needs to be done, and we
need to remove what does not belong into
the new land, the new consciousness, and
begin to see every single thing as part of us
and ourselves as a part of everything   with
no attachment; everything is in a complete
synchronicity with the universe, the
understanding of the cosmic consciousness.*

*There is this part of the authentic human
being that knows how to do this, and we*

*need to call upon this beautiful energy
inside of all life in Maya time (no time).*

*The authentic human being knows that
there is no separation in the energies of
male-female, that the inside is the same as
the outside, the knowledge of both in the
extreme make the whole circle, and the
complete and whole authentic human is
there; all is sacred. Only the connection
exists, and the essence of that connection is
love in the pure form.*

*For a long time we have been waiting for
this moment as a human being, a time where
all human beings are able to reach the
knowledge and understanding of Oneness.*

*For thousands of years many teachers
spoke about this time space, and they did
open the door for embracing perfection as a
human being; they have come to show us the*

11

ways of the spirit and the love in the perfect expression.

Our beautiful planet is moving, changing and with this dance that she is having the doors are opening again for the understanding to be embraced, but this time, a human being is her own savior; a human being is able to free herself from all boundaries and attachment, now she is able to perfect the love in the hearts and to enlighten that beautiful mind with that love that resides in the heart.

The awakening of the feminine knowledge has brought so many beautiful things, for we have, indeed, so many beautiful teachers before us that have shown us the way. For a long time they did remain hidden yet never forgotten; they were waiting for the time to come and be re-born in each woman and in each heart, for sacredness resides in all life forms, in everything that exists. And it is, indeed, the feminine with her love that brings the healing and the teachings into the male manifestation.

Magdala, Ix Xhel, Buffalo White Calf Woman, Quan Yin, Tara, Christ, Quetzatcoatl or Kukulcan, and so many others promised to come back and the promises have been honored, for we are, indeed, the knowledge and the heart of the oneness, as they showed in their teachings.

Can we recognize them inside of us? Then we are alive, too, as well as their teachings.

I am Magdala, a Maya-Mexica, yet this is a filter that I choose to live in this time space; we have many ceremonies and a very beautiful way of living through our traditions; our ways are indeed so beautiful, our knowledge is powerful, for we understood as a tribe the cycles of life and the universe and the energy of male-female bonding and dancing inside of each life force, for we understood that we belong to the mother so we honor her in every possible way, We also recognize as our knowledge taught us that in all the world, in the many tribes, resides also the same knowledge, for oneness is not only about one tribe, not only one kind of life form; oneness is in all the minerals, plants, animals, and also the other planets and the multiuniverse. Oneness is there for us to uncover, and it resides in the heart, we all are her-story, and we all are what the Great Spirit is. Perfection is always there.

Father teaches us his divine order; he did create laws that make all life forms live in peace and beauty in the cycles of life, and those laws were created because of the love of the mother, so all the creatures live in peace and perfect harmony. He is perfect,

*and all divine order is for creating
perfection.*

*The Mother teaches to us about love; she
is indeed the one who nurtures us and
provides us with the biggest miracle, the
miracle of love in the purity of expression.
There is no other kind of love, and love has
always been unconditional and resides in
each heart, in each essence, in the very
center, the place where all is created.*

*And together they dance, they dance and
they dance, and the dance turns into the
creation of many life forms, so love and
wisdom, the place of the creation and the
perfect manifestation is this dance that has
always been there. We need to recognize this
in our heart and in our mind, for this is the
time where the mind equals the heart.*

*For many years people have said that the
mind is a bad thing, well, I am telling you*

*that the mind is beautiful; human beings
need to learn how to use it and awaken the
mind. Awakening the mind can only be
performed by the heart, for the heart
enlightens the mind through the love and the
bonding that she has in herself. Teachings of
the feminine have been so guarded for such
a long time, and in so many ways are still
guarded, for there is so much power and
beauty in them.*

*I am a voice, a voice that is in your heart,
a voice that whispers inside of all life
beings, for this is the time for bringing back
the knowledge of the feminine ways, the
place where all creation takes place so our
manifestations are one and the same, for
only Oneness resides.*

*Now is the time to bring the heart into the
traditions or religions, for it is through the
heart that all traditions become alive and
beautiful; for a ceremony without the heart*

is empty, and the heart without the ceremony feels dull. I have not come here to destroy traditions or the male way; I have come here to consummate them.

In the very center of all tradition resides unity, the knowledge of oneness, just different ways of expression, but in that core, the center, and all traditions become one because of love.

Mama loves all her children, all the same, all are sacred, and she is calling, "come back to me", and this is a journey that must be performed by all true human beings and all life forms. She is calling and we are going back home to her call.

I am you

Magdala

Her Story

   *In ancient times there were temples,
schools that taught the ways of the feminine.
Those temples were in charge of the light of
the planet and women went there to study
and practice light, in all the manifestations
that are possible.*

   *Those temples were and still are in many
places of the world, China, Avalon, Maya,
Machupichu, Mexico, Egypt, Brazil, and
many other places. They are hidden because
the work they make is very deep; it is,
indeed, the Holy Spirit knowledge, an
understanding that has been hidden for
many centuries.*

   *Now the world is ready to embrace this
knowledge, the world is ready to listen into
their hearts and embrace sacredness in all
life, the world is very much begging for the*

*healing and the understanding of the most
powerful ceremony, the ceremony where the
two becomes one, at the place where only
sacredness resides.*

*Many girls in that time space were given
to those schools in order to find the work as
women, and it was a great honor for the
family if the girls were accepted in those
schools, for it is indeed the awakening of the
holy spirit within them, then light will lead
the way for the many.*

*Many practices were done, ceremonies
and healings, many teachings for the heart
of the woman who loves, the whole world
depended on those schools of enlightenment.*

*Women uncovered the way of giving
light to the men, and in that way all the
manifestation around them became holy, for
sacredness of all life is the way of the Holy
Spirit.*

*These woman were light givers for
everything around them became light, they
knew many realms of the consciousness,
many dimensions of the self.*

*The uncovering of the understanding of
the elements were part of the way of living,
sacred dance was understood as the way of
the heart, healing was performed as a
natural way through the awakening of the
love in the heart, dreaming woman
teachings were performed as an altered
state of consciousness by the understanding
of the virtual reality; there were many other
teachings. These women were in perfect
control of all their charkas, and in perfect
communion with the spirits in higher planes,
and in perfect harmony with the universe;
they understood the power that they have in
their wombs and the connection in a
complete form with all the dimensions.*

Oneness was the way of living, but this knowledge was not for everyone, it needed to be protected from the Gray people, or the archons, the ones that created the patriarchal system.

Many ancient temples were teachings of sacred sex and ceremonies for the awakening of light in the womb to enlighten all human kind; this is the teaching of the Holy Spirit.

Woman has the ability to open portals, she is a living vortex and the connection for higher dimensions, and she is the door for enlightenment. The man that was with this woman needed to be strong and wise and brave to receive that light. Many man died in the intent to receive the light because the struggle in their inner battle was too strong, the sensation is losing the self so that the ego can never be there. So it was prohibited to have sex with a regular man, the man

*needed to pass through several initiations
before he could be a candidate for this
woman. And one of these initiations was
going to the underworld, the place where the
fears are met.*

*Woman used to teach the man about sex.
Woman is the one who gives the manhood.
The phallus is given from the mother, and
the manhood is given from the enlightened
woman, a priestess, if they could handle all
the initiations. Even in these days a man
needs to pass through his gotlet (courting
time). It is a test that the men need to cross
and that still come from the spirit in natural
ways.*

*In that time, great women were there to
give their light to the men, Some of these
men were Thoth and Maat, Christ and
Magdala, Quetzalcoatl and Quetzalkina,
Pythagoras and his pitoniss, the same went
for Hermes, and many others, and all these*

women came from those schools. Even the Christ has said about these women...."if a man becomes a husband of one of these women the heaven is a promise for him".... They needed to be very brave!

When the patriarchal system was installed, they destroyed many of these temples, but some of these temples went into a higher dimension, for the knowledge cannot be destroyed, truth can never be destroyed.

During the destruction of the feminine ways, the men who could not embrace light went to kill, rape, and cut the women into pieces. Mutilation was there, mutilation for women started then; women still carry this pain.

Temples were destroyed, but knowledge has been hidden all this time, there are still so many things that cannot be said, but only one to one, in a very secret way.

After that destruction, came the distortion of the knowledge, whore houses became the schools for the man that we see now, and the "manhood" that comes from the system has become a warrior for the destruction of life, instead of the protector of life. Nowadays, women need to protect themselves from the protectors.

The patriarchal system massacres whatever feels feminine, for the feminine became a slave, the heart became enslaved, and all humanity entered in another dark age, that still is happening all over the world. But the time of slavery have been finished, now it is time to embrace freedom as the right given as a human being. Now is the time for the emerging of the feminine and her sacred work, to give light, once again, the manifestation.

Illusion of separation took place, a long time ago, the understanding as a way of living of Oneness became hidden in the heart of all living creatures. But it is there buried and humans need to dig and dig until they find oneness again as a way of living. What is found is the true self, the true human being.

Some of the women who survived from the temple's destruction became so afraid and angry with the men, the manifestation, that they began to have sex with each other, like in the island of Lesbos.

Nowadays, human beings have encountered a big distortion in their own ways to relate to themselves, and it is reflected in the sex, sex has become a big misunderstanding of using a divine energy.

Sex has been distorted by the patriarchal system, the patriarchal system wanted to destroy anything that would be able to free the people from slavery; they began to hide ancient codices that speak about this liberation, the feminine ways. But, sex is a very beautiful, powerful ceremony that will liberate, so the men have created a God in their own image, a God that has sex issues, a God that is male and hates women, and a God that considers women soulless. Furthermore, they have said that sex is a portal of darkness created by the woman and that sainthood comes with celibacy, the repression of sex.

Distortion came into being because of that, the harmony of nature was broken, wars and separation began and the environment and the planet Terra turned to chaos and many animals and plants that were there for healing purposes became extinct; human being's values broke into pieces, and sadness was everywhere. People forgot how to return into balance, how to dance with the Mother to go back into harmony. And it is a fear to speak about these things, still there is the silence, it is because in the his-story many people have been killed for this knowledge. Not too long ago, in the Inquisition, six million women were killed because of this knowledge. Of course, people are afraid to speak in the open, the teachings of sex, nowadays, are only spoken about in the physical realm, and still denying the energy, sex is only considered as a physical union to create pleasure in the body or for reproduction purposes but not to open doors for new realms within the self. There are so many worlds to discover.

There is a resentment about destroying the temples, but deep inside there is a space in the woman's heart that knows truth, but she is very afraid to find it. A woman is a temple, the altar in her must be found, the man is the prayer. And together they become one.

Feminine and Male Energy

Feminine energy represents the part of a human being that it is hidden, it is the virtual reality that takes place in very single life form, it is the essence and the force of life, for life, indeed, has many expressions, many forms.

Feminine is indeed the connection where all manifestation takes place; it is the place where the spirit resides, the Holy Spirit that embraces the oneness of the all.

Feminine is the essence of all vibration, she is indeed, the mystery.

Feminine carries all the memories of past life times as well all as the memories from this life. She remembers everything since the beginning of time, she is the story of all the

31

planet and the history, her-story, of the events, not just the ones created in a third dimensionality but all the dimensions at the same time. She remembers sensations, feeling, fears, love; she has the knowledge of the all.

Male represents the manifestation. Male way is the part of us that is able to perform and to create a reality according to the heart, according to his own feminine understanding.

Male is indeed the perfect manifestation of the father who creates the laws where all the life forms agree to live in perfect divine order. For all life forms have the understanding of divine order within themselves, in the outside realm, embracing the inside, their feminine, that holds oneness and always takes place as the beautiful expression of the divine.

Creation is always there, through the dance of the feminine-male, creation is performing every single minute. Because human beings are divine by nature, they are creators, they are in complete arrangement with the universe, and they will create in one way or the other.

Yet, as creators, human beings are going to create according to with their own feminine within themselves. If they do not understand or have a disconnection or distortion of the feminine, their creations will destroy life.

Female and male are the electromagnetic forces, they always go together, they cannot be separated, and one cannot be without the other, yet they are not equal in their nature.

Male represents the mind, female represents the heart, The mind holds all the cultural beliefs, programming, religion,

*language, religion, age, gender, the system;
mind works as deduction way and is
concrete.. Heart holds love, sensations,
experiences, spirituality, connection with the
spirit; heart holds inductive ways and is
abstract.*

*Because the third dimension is the realm
of duality, the mind is controlling the heart.*

$$M>H$$

Where M is mind and H is heart.

*In this realm, all is relative according to
the perception of the human being; human
beings will perceive the reality according to
their own beliefs and their past experiences.
In order to move human being from those
parameters, we must understand how mind
and heart work together; we truly want to
understand how these forces work within the*

self first, so we will be able to understand sacred sex.

We want to make Mind=Heart,

$$M=H$$

Cultural beliefs (religion, age, economic status, school , nationality, tradition or religion) +gender = M

Love + gender + experiences = H

Cultural belief is about time, process, evolution. It will change according to the "times".

Love and experiences also speak about time, but in another way; the heart will remember all past experiences and repeat them as an addiction, as a pattern because for the heart there is no time; the heart is in the same time space where those experiences took place; the heart will remember. This is the realm where beliefs are created, because of love.

Then if it is about time (t), and the mind needs a process and the heart keeps on desiring, longing, it will be a never ending battle. Stop fighting with yourself. Equality, balance is not there.

Now the planet is moving into the fifth dimension, in a realm where there is no time, that is why the understanding of male-female forces needs to be in balance, this is the very first door for many more dimensions, meaning that the cultural belief needs to grow into its evolution as much as the heart needs to go deep inside to the very center to unite with desire.

$$CB + (t) = L+(t)$$

CB-L = t/t

CB-L= One (t)

The time enters into oneness, a realm where time does not exist, is truly eternal momentum; in that realm only the mind will equal the heart. Male and female energies will be one and the same; the conscious and subconscious mind meet, so it ceases to exist, nothing is hidden, the realm where the cause and effect meet, without a process.

The space within the self, the heart does not recognize time as linear, knowing how to disconnect the process and bring the balance through the knowledge of non time. The heart truly will free the mind from a cultural belief that is only functioning through a process.

Sacred sex takes place in the heart of the sacredness within the self, even not being aware. Sacred sex is not a technique, it is an understanding, it is a way of living, it is the way of the spirit, as Christ said, to make the inside the same as the outside and the outside the same as the inside, for what it is in my heart, I will manifest. In order for sex to be sacred, sacred understanding must be there, in the altar, in the heart, in living in a sacred manner.

If you are looking for a technique, this is not the book for you.

Aztec Uroboros

Woman

For long time the men have referred to humanity as a male entity, woman was only an extension of the man, his rib. They referred to her only as possession of a man, a property, a thing that does not exist by her but only as a reflection of him. He began to masculinize her to fit in his ways, mold her into his needs, and even explain her woman nature only as a reference to him. For the men clitoris is only an "undeveloped phallus", even the word woman means a man with a womb, and she stayed in silence for all this time. But now, in the day of the woman, she has begun to stand up and say "I exist" and the shaking has begun.

Today, woman feels used by the man through sex. She has the need for giving light, and she has the passion of life inside

of her, so sex for her is a spiritual purpose.
Love is the way, so she is trying so hard to
find the right man for her, without
understanding the dance of the union of
polarities that it is taking place inside of
her.

Even if she is married, she has sorrow
because she has been mutilated in her own
feminine ways. She needed to hide her
feeling, powers and sensations; she needed
to communicate only what the male had
been imposing on her, whatever he was able
to understand in his own disconnected heart.
She needed to go into the male ways and
work in the male world, and hide herself,....
hide from herself.

A single woman, deep in her heart, is
in search for that man who will help her to
realize her sacredness as a woman. She
wants to be recognized with all her power as
a woman, not for the abilities to work in the

*system as a man, but for possibility to open
her inner core through love to a man whom
she wants so desperately to be worth it.*

*She needed to hide her power, too,
because the men felt challenged by her
power and did not accept a powerful woman
at his side.*

*She was denied as a gender, when the
patriarchal system imposed in the world,
that only what you can see or touch exists,
so love, heart ways, dimensionality and
many other rights of the human were denied.*

*In order to open herself, she must realize
that making love happens 24 hours a day,
she needs to trust her man one hundred
percent, she needs to feel appreciated in her
work as a woman, and she needs to
surrender completely to the spirit of love to
awaken that part in her that is the Holy
Spirit.*

*Sex has been so badly misunderstood;
the patriarchal system, the controllers, knew
exactly where to stop enlightenment for
humans and create all kinds of distortion for
sex.*

*The ones who created the program, the
wounded father, have created an image of
sex as a terrible act. In many religious, sex
has become a moral issue instead of a
realization of the self, and people have
become slaves because of the sex distortion
way of thinking in the system.*

*A woman embraces her womanhood the
very first time that she has her moon time; in
that magical moment, she begins to wonder
about sex. She begins to question herself and
her process for embracing her divinity as a
woman has begun.*

Woman in Sacred Dance in Belur India

*In many traditions, women have a
ceremony for welcoming the womanhood,
she is appreciated and honored as the true
daughter of the divine Mother, and her*

45

*Goddesshood has been awakened. Then, it
will be up to her to become one with herself.
And the ceremony is to help her in that
process.*

*Nowadays, these ceremonies have been
forgotten, there is no celebration and the
goddesshood has been lost, and
misunderstanding took place, and feminists
developed as another way of expressing the
male, for being a feminist is indeed a way
to become male instead of a celebration of
the feminine as the feminine in the purest
form, not as a reflection or comparison of
the male.*

*Feminism was a good way to start, yet
woman are not equal to men; women are
light givers, women are a channel of life, so
why ask for equality? Both polarities are
different, very different parameters to see
reality, besides; the struggle is not about the
men to grant them equality. The men do not*

*own the sacredness of the women. Women
need to remember what they are as a gender
and all the power that they have as women.*

*When a woman has sex for the very first
time, she immediately begins to feel
something is wrong, to feel she lost
something because of the system's ways of
thinking. An injection of profanity has
occurred instead of the most beautiful
experience of love.*

*In her light ways, she begins to search
for a man to share the light that resides in
her womb, and her search can continue all
her life without realizing that all is inside of
her.*

*And every time, she is in that search for the
one who is able to embrace her in her
totality, she gets more tangled inside of
herself, because every man's energy that*

has been inside of her remains there, and she is not aware of it, she just feels him.

Women will transform, transmute everything. Women will transform the energy the man gives, whatever manifestation gives, whatever he has, through her open portal to receive whatever he can afford in exchange for that energy. In other words, feminine will transmute all the experiences and energies that she goes through in life, and it is draining her life force.

There are many issues that the woman thinks are hers that don't belong to her; they belong to the man who has been inside of her womb. If the man feels that he needs to possess, to take with anger, or to use whatever distortion that he has about the "manhood", she will carry that energy in her, thinking that she is the one who needs

*to work with that issue, as the patriarchal
system makes her think.*

*She feels dishonored and possessed; she
can't think of anything else but that man
who has been inside of her. She thinks it
must be love because she does not
understand what really took place, yet deep
inside of her, she knows something is wrong.
She has become a slave of his issues and
hers. Unless she is aware of it and makes a
ceremony to take him out, he will be there as
a spiritual parasite taking her power away.*

*Then she feels desperate and tries to go
for another man to be inside of her, who will
make her forget the first man. The need for
love is so intense that she will try over and
over again to be recognized, and she will get
more tangled. Then pain comes; she feels
separated and disintegrated within herself,
and she needs to put herself together again,
even when she does not understand what is*

happening in her. She begins to feel like she is a lesser woman and her image becomes poor. She begins to feel "I am not good enough" because she has not been recognized as a sacred being of light. Then, she begins to feel so disconnected within herself and begins to compete with other woman.

But she will find the way of integrating herself, through the sisterhood, through her own heart and through the connection with the Great Mother inside of herself.

Coyolxauhqui, She was also called one who
"spoke to all the centipedes and spiders and
transformed herself into a sorceress" or a
"very evil woman".

Man

The man, on the other hand, feels "I am not a good enough...man..." because my mother, lovers, heart, father, religion, system said so. The patriarchal system, the wounded father, has told him that he is not responsible for anything in his life that only the system will protect him, and he believes in that.

The man feels that he needs to prove himself to feel worthy and believes that through war and destruction he can find his worthiness. He feels so disconnected by the woman he fears that he has tried to destroy himself and the planet in all the possible forms. His own disconnection to the feminine and his lack of knowledge of love and sex has brought him in to a big despair.

What he really wants, what he really longs for, is to go back into the womb, the place where he received his sacred phallus, the light that comes from the spirit, the place where he comes from. He longs for somebody to trust him, to love him, to rebirth him, to enlighten him, to give him life again and again…and again.

He needs to embrace the true man, the true human being within himself, where his sacredness resides. But he feels that there is no archetype to show him the way. A man needs to have a reflection in the outside to click in the inside. The archetypes that the men have about manhood are soldiers, war games, and sexual attitudes in the controlling ways. He learns to see aggression as a male attribute, as well as conquistador and ruler.

He does not see himself as a protector of life, the manifestador of beauty and peace, the one who embraces the divine order in all the living things, he has forgotten his position in the universe.

The emerging feminine is a threat for him. He feels that he must share his power and does not understand that the sacred woman will enlighten him, he is obsessed with power, in the only realm where the illusion of power resides, the third dimension, so he wants to keep the linear way of thinking so he can be in control. He is afraid. The patriarchal system is afraid because his days are counted.

Enlightenment means In-light, light from within, to receive the light from the inside light. We live in a world of light, our bodies are light, there is only light. In-lighten is always there inside of each light.

Awareness means to be conscious about it; it means to enlighten the male side. This

*means no more battle between subconscious
and conscious, only light through unity.*

*A man will accept as much light from her
as he accepts light from his own feminine
side. As much peace as he has within himself
is as much light as he will receive. This
peace can be disturbed by what he feels is
"the monster".*

Xolotl, Aztec male archetype, the
trickster.

The Saint and the Whore

For I am the first and the last.
I am the honored one and the scorned one.
I am the whore and the holy one.
I am the wife and the virgin.
I am <the mother> and the daughter.
I am the members of my mother.
I am the barren one

          and many are her sons.
I am she whose wedding is great,

        and I have not taken a
        husband.
I am the midwife and she who does not bear.
I am the solace of my labor pains.
I am the bride and the bridegroom,

        and it is my husband who
        begot me.

This is an excerpt from " The Thunder, the Perfect Mind", written by Mary of Magdala.

Magdala has been considered for hundreds of years the perfect representation of the whore.

For a long time she has been hidden inside of the woman just waiting to be uncovered, and this is happening in a beautiful way; women in the world need Magdala to begin to embrace the sacredness of the feminine in order for Magdala to be awakened, and in order to redeem herself in the consciousness of the world, not as the whore, but as the sacred wife of the Christ, the Saint.

Mary of Magdala according Leonardo Da Vinci

In the process of rediscovering herself, a woman has suffered in her inner core the shame of being a whore; she feels she has prostituted herself in all the forms that the male ways were willing to provide to her. She also feels that about her own mother who helped her for that prostitution, as an

image of herself, for generations. Why?
Because her mother, in her inner core was
in silence too. She was loving in a deep
manner, but she was not being understood,
and she did want her daughter to survive
until the time came to speak ; she wanted
her daughter to be safe, so she taught her to
remain in silence as much as she could and
make pain a virtue in order to survive.
Mothers remember the time where the
women were killed when they were
performing their womanhood. Pain is
stronger than the Mother's true teachings,
women are afraid to follow the Great
mother's teachings.

In the history of her wound and
rediscovering herself, a woman has been
selling herself in all the possible ways, just
for the illusion of love. For love still has not
been uncovered from the space of the
sacredness, but only through a manifestation
of a cultural belief, an attachment that only

reflects the heart in the pollution of the whore.

Yet, behind that whore resides the most magnificent force. Being able to love in the most perfect manner in the expression, she gives herself with the perfect surrender that a divine being can express. So, she exists indeed, not for only the pleasure of the body, but to realize the ecstasies of the enlightened as a divine force.

She is, indeed, and has always been, the perfect manifestation of true love in motion; in her dance she has found herself and her position in the world. She is, indeed, the bridge of love.

She feels guilty because her lack of understanding of her own sexuality. For having the capacity of love eternally, she feels that she is a whore always looking for love, she feels that she needs to disconnect

*herself from the heart for so many times that
she has been hurt, and she also becomes
afraid to love in a deep manner, in a
surrender to the spirit ways of love, in a way
that she knows what love is. She knows the
way of surrender into the spirit of love, so
she waits in silence to be discovered again,
for her own consciousness allows the
healing of her heart and brings her heart
back into her own true being. In other
words, she is waiting in the outside world
for a man capable of understanding and
embracing her in a complete manner, to
accept her as a woman, not as a reflection of
the man as the Lilith but as a true sacred
woman, the Eve inside of her. The Lilith
and the Eve now are united; the whore and
the saint are one.*

*The "holy whore" is capable of bringing
the most powerful reality that a human
being can reach, for she is indeed a channel
of the spirit and can bring a true human*

being into a new reality. Now she, the sacred woman, is giving birth to the new world.

In her womb resides the most powerful force, that, when connected into true love opens an incredible vortex through that realization, and everything is changed. She will open a vortex, new realities, in one way or the other because she is, indeed, the bridge of the spiritual world.

Women are giving birth to the fifth dimension, the new world.

The whore and the Saint Aztec Codex

She has been called whore by the patriarchal system, the patriarchal system wanted to destroy her, her powers, and her children, because they were so afraid of the mystery, afraid of the power of the Holy Spirit. But she has survived; she has a new understanding now and is ready to make her work. She once was the whore, now she has become the holy.

For life times she has been waiting for this moment, a moment to be recognized, as she truly is, she is now the woman who recognizes her dance of the seven veils, not the seven demons that the patriarchal system wanted to use and abuse.

A woman who loves in the true way, in her own recognition, will be redeemed through the dance of love that she is already performing or that she is willing to perform because it is in her inner way of recognizing herself as the daughter of the Great Mother.

'Sophia' of the Essenes, Gnostics and early Christians has a central role:

*For the woman is the crown of man, and the
final manifestation of humanity.
She is the nearest to the throne of God, when
she shall be revealed.
But the creation of woman is not yet
complete: but it shall be complete in the time
which is at hand.
All things are thine, O Mother of God: all
things are thine, O Thou who risest from the
sea; and Thou shalt have dominion over all
the worlds.*

…and the time is NOW…

*There are many writings in many cultures,
for many have passed on the knowledge of
the feminine in silence to the daughters of
the Great Mother, from generation to
generation, waiting for "the moment", the
moment of the day of the woman.*

The same knowledge is all over the world; the Geishas in Japan, they also have the same knowledge, the whore and the saint, the knowledge hidden, the Tao, written by Laoma, but signed by her husband, when she was considered his mistress, the feminine way.

The Mayan and Aztec "calendar" guided by the moon cycle, is a feminine knowledge; Avalon and many other cultures have hidden this knowledge for such a long time…just waiting for the time…

And the time is now, for the women have grown to embrace their own sacredness, the sacredness of life that it is giving birth to the new word.

The Monster

There is a program that says, never receive from a woman... nothing can be good if it comes from a woman....sex is a bad thing. Women have no soul, women are is good only to have children, and God is male. So he broke his heart by disconnecting himself from his own heart, his feminine side.

However, this program can be destroyed from the inside out and from the outside in through love.

For a man, his first encounter with a woman was his mother, so the relationship with other women will depend very much in that first encounter. He has been inside of her womb, receiving her love, her light, and life, she was the channel from the spirit to bring him into this realm, and there are so many things that depend on her.   If it was a clear woman with unconditional love for him, and him willing to receive, he will never lose the connection with the spirit, so he will have good relation with the woman in his life. He will never dishonor or hurt any woman, and he will understand in his inner heart the sacredness of life that the woman represents in this planet. He will learn to surrender and make the prayer of love inside of her as the temple that she is; love always finds the way. On the contrary, if the mother had disconnection within herself, a woman that has been hurt, she will send this energy to her children, and the boy who has been hurt by the mother will try to revenge himself in every single woman that he meets, and he will try to hurt them, and control them, and possess them because of the power that a woman has in him and because he was hurt.

Men truly recognize the power of the women but they are afraid of it because they do not understand where they come from.

Deep inside men recognize that a woman is a creature of love and innocence, a life giver from the spirit. She is the mystery and he is afraid of her.

In the system men have learned many ways to dishonor women. One way is to try to conquer them in order to possess; that is why many wars started. The fight was the land, the woman's heart, to break the mystery in them, to conquer the mystery world. The battle was about how much land they "possess", but land is not for sale, land can never be possessed. Human beings are just passing through it, land can never be conquered. The only thing to be conquered is the self, the ego.

When a man has hurt a woman that hurt will be in his aura. Another woman will feel it in her spirit, and she will know he is a woman hurter, so as unity works, woman knows that he is not the man for receiving the light, He will never get it, unless healing takes place.

A man feels the monster, he feels ashamed of himself, he feels the Xolotl, the trickster, and he is very afraid to be uncovered. He is so afraid of the feminine that he will hide any emotion, anything that can reflect who he truly is, who he thinks he is.

Men represent the consciousness, women are enlightening the consciousness.

A woman remembers all her lovers; and every time she remembers a bad experience she will curse him. That curse will follow him forever until forgiveness is done.

But, how does the man relate with the whore-saint? Deep inside, the man can relate with the whore, because he has become a whore in himself; he loves the whore, the part of a woman that is willing to sell herself. She will beg for love over and over and will do what it takes to retain the men manipulating and controlling him in all possible ways, she will use the power in a wrong way to control him because her need for love is almost unbearable. He loves her because it is the way he relates inside of himself, the only language of love that he recognizes as a man. But deep inside, he longs for the one who is the "virgin" the one who is indeed, a true lover, who is willing to teach him the true ways of love, the true ways of a human being, but he fears her so much and hates himself for not having the courage to love her in a deep manner.

He thinks about a woman the way he relates to himself in the heart. He always wants to control and posses his own heart, until his heart becomes silent, so hurt, then he finds a woman who it is the perfect reflection of himself. She makes the man feel less guilty because she also has silenced her own connection to the spirit, the saint, the sacred place, and only provides him the pleasures of the body, the only way and the only space that he feels he can conquer. But true love is not his field, true love is a scary place for him, the "monster" as he sees himself, and so he does not allow this space in his heart to be healed. He is so completely afraid of love that he becomes crippled of his own spirituality, for he has cut his heart off because of fear.

Many sicknesses have come for the men because of this disconnection. A large percentage of the men are beginning to have prostate cancer, kidneys problems, impotence, premature ejaculation, and many others, sicknesses that are speaking about that disconnection with his own feminine inside. There is much guilt involved, so men are trying to find remedies to solve the problem in the outside without realizing the true problem, their own fear of love.

Yet, the man is really begging for the saint to rescue him, to put back his heart, to teach him how to love. The women are very much teachers of love, and he does understand that he has missed many lessons of love in his life in the patriarchal system. But with the sacred woman, he is willing to embrace himself fully.

*Healing, the Whore and the
Monster...*

*Sacred sweat lodge, Temazcalli, purification
place,   Aztec Codex.*

In ancient times, temazcalli, sweat lodge, inipi, were made for purification as part of a wedding ceremony, to ask the Great Spirit, for the blessing of the union and help them to overcome any kind of separation.

Men, nowadays, because of ignorance, have taken the power of the women. Every time that he wants to conquer, to control, to manipulate, to play games, with the love that she wants to offer him, he tangles himself more.

The ancients in our tribe said, "you never dishonor a cave, (woman) if you do, you will never reach enlightenment". In other words, "you don't fight with the cook otherwise you will be hungry."

For a man, healing must be made, a forgiveness journey for all the women in his life, including his mother. For they have been teachers for him without him realizing, and he has not honored their teachings.

Women are the bridge of love and his own salvation. In other words, your own heart is your own salvation. "Make the inside the same of the outside and the outside the same of the inside."

Sex has become a way to manipulate, control, abuse, and use other people. The true meaning has been forgotten.

Woman needs to remember and heal herself from the pain of separation. She, needs to stop competing with other woman, for in every woman is a sister; what is happening to one is happening to the many; then, the sisterhood is built.

The patriarchal system uses a very old trick to control and manipulate the primal force of enlightenment; "divide and conquer" has been used into this matter.

The pain of the woman is like if you have been bitten by a dog, you will be afraid of all the dogs, not just that one. If you hurt one dog, all the dogs will know that you are a dog hurter. They will be afraid of you, and the relationship will never grow until there is a healing for it.

A woman needs to find her own temple and altar to be able to find her courage for love again, to fully love again the way the Great Mother Loves, the Eternal Feminine that it is within herself. She must go into a journey to find her own male side and unify herself and understand that she is the one who brings her own reality, her own salvation through the Goddess of Love that she is. She must do that journey before she is in front of a man with all her power as a woman, using her medicine, even when he is

*not able to recognize her, she must be able
to recognize herself as she is, a Sacred
temple, a Light giver, a Holy entity ready for
love, the only language that she understands
in her inner core.*

*Women have many powers that they are
uncovering in themselves. For every relation
that they have, there is a power that was
given as a right for being women.*

*Human beings are ready to remember,
ready to understand the true meaning of
love and surrender, the purpose of life and
the connection with all the worlds inside and
out. A human being is a multidimensionality
being, having the ability to travel into many
worlds, and the only way to get there is
through love from the heart of the spirit.*

*Sacred love is not a technique; it is not a
path to follow in the outside world. Within
the human being is the path for their own*

redemption, their own enlightenment as they embrace themselves as human beings and surrender to the spirit. Whit this surrender love will open the door for a new world within them.

Healing is truly recognizing the true human being inside of the self.

The Sacred Temple

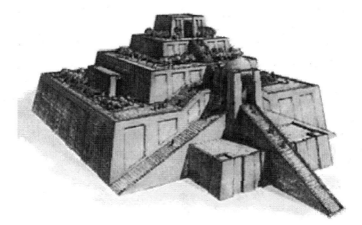

*Ziggurats, Sumerian ancient temples where
Father and Mother meet.*

*There has been a big controversy about
these temples, they have discovered 32, and*

they relate these temples with the Tower of Babel.

Chandela Temple in India

When the gray people took control in this planet and created the patriarchal system, bringing unbalance and chaos, they wanted to be sure that human beings never discovered their own self and the light that resides within the divine self.

The male oriented society that has brought the robotization of the human being is an energy inside of humans that wants to stop humans to discover themselves and their own greatness.

Humans are divine creatures, born from divinity, born from the love of the father-mother, born from the union of polarities. Human beings are not born from "sin"; they are beautiful and perfect as are the Mother and Father.

Balance has always been inside of all life forms by nature, but human beings have accepted the unbalance as a way of living,

87

as a program from the wounded father, the system, but deep inside is the understanding that there is much more.

Human beings do understand that behind each filter or wrong belief there is the truth that will connect directly into the center.

Our ancestors knew this very well; they understood that making love was about the surrender to the spirit and the power of love.

Man understood that making love was entering in a sacred place, the place where the man becomes God. Reverence, offerings, ceremonies, heart songs, needed to be done as a preparation for that encounter, and once there, at the temple, the true prayer was performed through the heart.

True love, sacredness in the sex is a vibration that involves all the chakra's alignment, being in full presence of the self, loving in a complete manner, trusting in a complete manner, being willing to die and being reborn with surrender to the spirit in a complete manner.

It involves the focus of the heart as the doorway to heaven.

Ancient Codex

In many tribes, the knowledge of sacred sex was there in so many ancient codices.

The knowledge of Christ and Magdala and their work about sacred sex is the root of the understanding.

This is a recollection of paragraphs from the Nag Hamadi, and other gnostic ancient writings that speak about the bride and the bridegroom, and of course the bridal chamber.

"Great is the mystery of marriage! For without it, the world would not exist"

The mystery of union is, indeed, the force of feminine-male together that makes life possible, it is, indeed, the essence of all life form and the manifestation in a perfect agreement and understanding that truly makes life sacred. Marriages of these forces create life and everything that exists, for the male represents the manifestation, but in the feminine is where the power of creation resides.

It is the mystery resolved and embraced when in oneself completed and when the marriage of both has been consummated, her-his inner, and her-his outer have become one. Then it is possible to make that unity with another human being who is willing to embrace unity in the maximum expression, the endless dance of the sacredness of life.

"Adorn yourself as a bride awaiting her bridegroom so that you may be what I am and I may be what you are. Place the seed of Light in your bridechamber. Receive the bridegroom from me and contain him and be contained by him. Behold, grace has come upon you." (38)

The sacred place where everything becomes one, the place where time does not

exist for human beings have become in-
lighted, for human beings have embraced
and recognized freedom as the eternal
divine right.

The bridal chamber is where the miracle
takes place, it is the recognition of the true
daughter of the great mother, the true son of
the great father, the perfect bonding of the
great spirit; all is contained in the one and
the one is being contained in the whole.
Wholeness, holiness, has been reached.
Grace is upon you....

"As spirit Mother, she is not, like the
Great Mother of the lower phase, interested
primarily in the infant, the child, the
immature man who clings to her in these
early stages...[she] governs the

transformation from the elementary to the spiritual level...[she] <u>*desires whole men knowing life in all its breadth*</u>*." (42)*

This is, indeed, the goddess in all her splendor, she is recognizing herself as the daughter of the Great Mother, and she truly wants a true man for herself. She will transform the boy into a beautiful man.

By her recognition, she is indeed, willing to conceive a man; she is there for his consummation as a human being. She is not interested in the boy with his attachments with the mother; she is there to fulfill him in his inner core.

She is transforming the boy into the man who knows life in all its breadth.

"Virginity implies that this Light is pure and intact".

    Virginity resides in the heart, virginity cannot be removed, be stolen,… unless the self agrees, nobody can remove something that belongs to you since the beginning of life.

    "Light is pure and intact" as the essence of god-dess, means that love is the perfect expression because the connection with the divinity is there. It is also related to the essence, just before the love in the expression, it is only light.

The bridal chamber is hidden. It is the Holy of Holies. The veil at first concealed how God arranged the creation, but when the veil is rent, the things inside are revealed.., this Ark will be its salvation."
(Philip 84: 20-35)

Yes, the Bridal Chamber is hidden inside of all human beings, and it is holy; it is the place where the virtual and the real become one, the place of creation. Many secrets are being revealed in that chamber. The Holy Sprit resides there.

"It is certainly necessary that they should be born again through the image. What is the resurrection? The image must rise again through the image. The bridegroom

and the image must enter <u>through the image into truth</u>.'' (Philip 67:15-20)

What is image? Human beings live in the world of images, everything they see, they see through a filter. That filter was created by cultural beliefs, ways of living, memories, everything that truly limits the true perception. The truth resides in the heart of all human beings, hidden, and what human beings see is on the image that they have within themselves.

Human beings need to recognize truth, to learn how to see beyond the eyes that lie, the eyes that are just so in love of an image. Image is a creation, the manifested world. When a human being is able to see beyond the images, he-she is ready to embrace his-her own true self with the eyes that can see the truth in the nakedness, see through the veil..

The bridegroom, our consciousness, our cultural beliefs, our manifested bodies, must enter into the truth, the essence of all, the place where everything becomes one, the bridal chamber.

Recognizing the self in the purest form means that human beings is able to contemplate the creation as it is in the perfect divine order.

"Truth did not come into the world naked, but it came in types and images." (67: 10)

This is indeed so beautiful, truth is always there, truth can be found only by the ones who can see themselves in the nakedness, for only a true heart can uncover truth and live in that way.

In this statement, the human being's spiritual work is shown.

"Light and darkness, life and death, right and left...are inseparable. (but) neither are the good good, nor the evil evil...each one will dissolve into its original nature. But those who are exalted above the world are indissoluble, eternal." (Philip 53:10—25)

There is no separation, there is only oneness; there is no limitation of the mind, or mind games, and there is only the essence of all life forms.

This is the space where ignorance does not exist; there is no more control, manipulation, separation, religions or cultural beliefs, only the perfection of surrender into the spirit. It is the space where everything and anything becomes one, the perfect vessel, the emptiness where it is being fulfilled by the spirit.

When Eve was still with Adam, death did not exist. When she was separated from him, death came into being. If he enters again and attains his former self, death will be no more.

Eve is the Holy Spirit, it is the realm of the true human being, the realm where enlightenment resides, where sacredness resides, and in that realm, there is no death or separation. Adam, the consciousness, the manifested world, what we think of ourselves into that separation must enter again with her, so death will be no more. Recognizing the sacredness of the self and living in that truth is where the Adam and Eve reside.

Eve attempts to awaken Adam to spiritual illumination, she says:

"I am the thinking of the <u>virginal spirit</u>... Arise and remember, and follow your root,

which is I...and beware of the deep sleep."
(Ap. John 31:10-20)

I am " thinking", thought, is the way of manifestation, it is in the place where the essence of all resides, the root, the principle creator, and it comes as an intention. She is thinking in the virginal spirit; the virginal spirit is pure and intact, she must connect first with this energy within herself.

That essence is the purity, calling upon the Manifestation, saying it is time to stand up and follow where you come from, to find the essence within the self, From that place she is calling, but also she is warning: beware of the deep sleep.

The awakened soul is the one that recognizes sacredness in the all.

A person who is still asleep is in separation and is not capable to enter into the bridal chamber.

In the bridal chamber opposites meet in God, represented by Light and Will:

"It belongs not to desire but to the will. It belongs not to the darkness or the night, but to the day and the light...Those who are separated will be united (and) will be filled. Every one who will enter the bridal chamber will kindle the light, for it turns just as in marriages...(observed) at night...But the mysteries of this marriage

are perfected *rather in the day and in the*
light. Neither that day not its light ever sets.
" (82.5—86.5)

In the bridal chamber, at the place where
the nakedness of the soul resides, it is not a
desire from the body, but the knowledge, the
understanding of the two who becomes one.

The bridal chamber is a portal, a portal
that must be understand and honored,
opening doors for many dimensions, and
each individual understanding will open
those doors. Really, human beings do not
want to open doors for nasty spirits.

If anyone becomes a son of the bridal
chamber, he will receive the Light. If
anyone does not receive it while he is in

these places, he cannot receive it in the other place." (Philip 86:5-7)

The Womb is a sacred place.

"It is because of the chrism that Christ has his name...he who has been anointed possesses everything...the resurrection, the light, the cross, the Holy Spirit. The Father gave him this in the mystery of the bridal—chamber

Valentinian* formula: "What liberates is knowledge of who we were, what we became; where we were, where into we have

*been thrown; whereto we speed, wherefrom
we are redeemed; what birth is, and what
rebirth. . . ."*

The Christ expresses in a beautiful way:

*"When you make the two one, and when you
make the inside like the outside and the
outside like the inside, and the above like the
below, and when you make the male and the
female one and the same, so that the male
not be male nor the female female; and
when you fashion eyes in the place of an eye,
and a hand in place of a hand, and a foot in
place of a foot, and a likeness in place of a
likeness; then will you enter the kingdom."*

Solomon as many others found his enlightenment though the love of the feminine.

4 For it is she that teacheth the knowledge of God, and is the chooser of his works.

In Philip's Gospel we also find beautiful knowledge about Male and Female Union.

Philip Gospel

When Eve was still with Adam, death did not exist. When she was separated from him, death came into being. If he enters again and attains his former self, death will be no more

*A bridal chamber is not for the animals nor
is it for the slaves , nor for defiled women
but it is for free men and virgins.*

*Through the Holy Spirit we are indeed
begotten again, but we are begotten through
Christ in the We are anointed through the
Spirit. When we were begotten , we were
united. None can see himself either in water
or in a mirror without light . Nor again can
you see in light without mirror or water. For
this reason, it is fitting to baptize in the two,
in the light and the water. Now the light is
the chrism.*

*If the woman had not separated from the
man she should not die with the man His
separation became the beginning of death.
Because of this, Christ came to repair the
separation, which was from the beginning,
and again unite the two and to give life to
those who died as a result of the separation ,
and unite them But the woman is united to*

*her husband Indeed, those who have united
in the bridal chamber will no longer be
separated . Thus Eve separated from Adam
because it was not in the bridal chamber
that she united with him*

– The Gospel of Philip

*The Eve and the Lilith, the whore and the
saint; a woman needs to become one with
her, unify these forces within her. How do
you unify these forces?*

*The Eve is where your sacredness
resides, Eve is the daughter of the Great
Mother; she has all the power that the
mother has, she is the divine inside of all
life, she is a voice that is inside of you, she
is your teacher and guide, she always looks
for your highest good and others, she loves
as only a divine can love, she is your higher
self and she is Your other you.*

The Lilith is the part of you that holds the teachings of the system. She competes, flirts with every single men, she manipulates and controls, she is the whore, she will sell herself and others and want other woman to get hurt, too, because it makes her feel less miserable, she is not happy and does not want anybody to be happy, she loves third dimensionality, she loves the comfort zone so she can be in control, she loves material things, she is not capable of love, she is a victim, she always makes excuses and blames everybody. It is the part of a woman that the system feeds, so it has been growing, and she is your other you.

Observe both of them, what they think, how they get fed, what they want, then choose. If you choose your sacredness, then observe the Lilith part, hunt her, but never attack her directly; she always wants to be a victim and will trick you. Stop feeding her,

111

stop her thoughts and listen to our
sacredness, your real teacher.

Mayan-Aztec ancient codices

Symbol of Omeceotl, male-female energies.

For long time those ancient codices have been waiting patiently for the people to be ready to listen, and still there is so much that cannot be said, or exposed, but the ancient ones left behind many traces for the ones who are hungry of the spirit and who are ready to uncover in themselves the deepest secrets. For there is in the heart of all humans the connection with the spirit, for all are connectors through all creation in this time and all the times, for time does not exist. It is the space in the inside where only eternal momentums exist and coexist.

Omeceotl, the first God that created all the gods, Omeceotl, is the energy of Male and Female together. This is the Aztec Mayan concept of unity.

Omeceotl is the Creator of all the Gods, for she-he is indeed the divine principle of all life forms and all the expression. It is the human being's spiritual purpose to be in the land of Omeceotl, when she-he make the inside the same of the outside and the outside the same of the inside.

Another way of expressing Omeceotl

Sex in the Mayan and Aztec and many other Native American tribes, as well as many other tribes in the world, was a sacred understanding, a way to connect father sky and mother earth.

There were Temples in Aztec and Mayan lands dedicated for sacred sex ceremonies, and, of course, many other tribes have special temples for this ceremony. The woman wait on top of the pyramid, all prepared for love, while the man moves up, step by step, having his initiations that will prepare him for love.

In most of the pyramids in Mexico, it is found the sacred knowledge of the sacred sex unity of love, a big phallic rock in the middle of circular stones, representing Father and

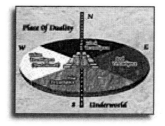

Mother ways of creation. The medicine wheel's knowledge came with this understanding as well as many others, like many worlds were discovered; Maya and Aztec found many dimensions that now Quantum physics are uncovering again.

There are many more ancient codices that explain this knowledge; nowadays, quantum physics explains the same knowledge, it shows us how the realities are being created. This "new" understanding will transform the world.

Love

…But everything starts because of love…

What is love?

There were ceremonies that in many ways are still being performed, the ceremony of a deep understanding of love and the expression of love. Do we need to separate expression and heart?

Sacred love is living life in a sacred manner, for whatever you go, you are standing in a sacred land, you make the land sacred through your presence; everything that you touch becomes alive when the touch is in a sacred manner.

True human beings understand the difference between love and sacred love as a way of living. For human beings understand love without any attachment, and then the understanding of Oneness unfolds in the heart.

Love is a divine right; only true humans are able to embrace and recognize love in the sacred manner, for all the relations are sacred in the heart of the true human being.

All relations come from the realm of love; human beings have learned to love a big spectrum of relationships, yet they feel that it is because of the relation that love happens, without understanding that the heart has, indeed, many mansions, many ways of expressing the same thing, yet it comes from the very center of the heart; all love is truly sacred, as is all relations.

Love has always been the way for the true human way of living, love in the purest expression is without the attachment; attachment comes from pain of separation that the mind creates an ego form to separate, segregate, and control love.

Love is a force that cannot be controlled and it is in the divine nature unconditional, there has never been such a thing as conditional love; love has its own ways for the heart always wants to be expressed in the purest form, without infiltrations or limitations or conditions that will create pain through the attachment.

Love heals everything, for it is the divine force within the self that purifies, makes things pure and innocence, but indeed has many expressions.

Human beings heal all the relations through love; because of love human beings can reach the maximum realization of the self.

In the sacred place of love in the heart of human beings resides the power of the divine in all the expression because it is the essence of all expression.

Human beings came as teachers of love; they are born with complete surrender, and the mother awakens the most powerful expression of love that has been inside of her as her divine right.

Love can never be separated, for the essence is one and oneness is all what it is, love is truly divine.

Sacred Sex

Sacred Marriage, from Aztec codex

From Hermes Trimegisto

*Separate that spirituous earth from the
dense or crude by means of a gentle heat
with much attention.*

*In great measure it ascends from the earth
up to heaven, and descends again, newborn,
on the earth, and the superior and the
inferior are increased in power.*

*By this wilt thou partake of the honours of
the whole world. And Darkness will fly from
thee.*

*This is the strength of all powers. With this
thou wilt be able to overcome all things and
transmute all what is fine and what is
coarse.*

– Hermes Trismegistus

Beautiful Hermes describes sacred sex in the male way, the work of the men, in such a beautiful manner.

Separate that spirituous earth from the dense or crude by means of a gentle heat with much attention

Separate from the "Monster", the Xolotl energy, remove your ego so love can flow as it is in your nature; be present, stay present in the love, in that precious eternal moment. Gentle heat, not a burning all, but be in the gentleness and allow the heat to be through love, stay focused in the love.

When the ceremony of sacred love takes place, man does not ejaculate. Semen is the life force, it is sacred. He will loose his own life when he ejaculates, he holds his energy in order to receive the light, and if he ejaculates he will loose his energy; he will

*loose connection to the spirit. Reverse the
flow as the ancestors have said many times.
The focus in the love that he has gives him
the control of himself that he needs to
perform the surrender; it is very much
controlling without ruling, without
imposing, without possession, but allowing
harmony to happen, She needs that energy
in order to open herself and give light.*

*In great measure it ascends from the earth
up to heaven, and descends again, newborn,
on the earth, and the superior and the
inferior are increased in power.*

   *In the connection with the spirit of love,
the snake, the kundalini, the feminine
energy, the Earth, will ascend up to heaven,
your crown chakra, and the men and women
will be re-born. This is call the second birth
and both will increase in power because*

both have made the connection in the spirit and created the vortex that open the doors of the new beautiful world.

By this wilt thou partake of the honours of the whole world. And Darkness will fly from thee

This is the right that all human beings have; the right of their enlightenment and there is no place for darkness in the light.

This is the strength of all powers. With this thou wilt be able to overcome all things and transmute all what is fine and what is coarse.

The strength is unity; there is where the power resides, in the male-female energies

*together. This is the way to transmute all
what is needed to be transmuted.*

*Hermes found his enlightenment
through a beautiful Pitoniss, a sacred
woman who opened the doors for him. Yet
he did a lot of initiations to open the heart.*

From Tao Te Ching

*The "Valley Spirit"
The Valley Spirit never dies
It is named the Mysterious Female.
And the doorway of the Mysterious Female
Is the base from which Heaven and Earth
sprang.
It is there within us all the while;
Draw upon it as you will, it never runs dry.*

Making Love is entering in the Valley of the Spirit, with so much gentleness and love; it is the sacred place where the two become one, the place where Heaven and Earth meets, the place of Oneness.

The Valley of the Spirit is the woman's body, the valley that never dies is the vagina that never gets dry, it is the door of the mystery, the place where heaven and earth sprang; this is the water of life, the water that never ends.

In the place where everything becomes one, she is the Goddess, the light giver, she is in her own realm, she has authority, she detaches herself from all the boundaries and limitations; it is her world. Uniting with all things, she is completely fulfilled. She is the tree of life.

I wanted to start with those descriptions, for both are very beautiful; sacred sex is not a technique, it is a spiritual work by two people who love each other so much and want to express themselves for their own enlightenment. There is no way that man and woman can make love ceremony without a deep spiritual work.

There is so much in this matter that cannot be said or explained in a book, for it is a deep spiritual practice that for a long time has been hidden; there are many books that talk about sacred sex, but still there is not the ways of the woman being spoken. It needs to be hidden because there is still so much darkness in the world that will take this knowledge and control and manipulate with it and hurt many women and children. But I can say what it is permitted at this time, and please, understand that the ancestors of the many tribes did many initiations that nowadays are very much

impossible to perform because people are
not ready for those beautiful initiations.
There is so much fear, anger, and
separation to overcome before even being a
candidate for these initiations.

Sacred Sex is a powerful understanding
of the union of polarities; it all starts with
unifying the self, both forces, male and
female in perfect balance.

Today there is so much sexual stimulus
that a man cannot control himself;   then, he
will try to control everything that he can,
well, to have the illusion of control.

The system has taught the man that a
sexual encounter is about ejaculation, that
the relationship to have with a woman
involves only the lower chakras; he has been
taught that the purpose of sex is ejaculation
and control of the feminine. He thinks this is
a way of showing his aggressiveness and

dominion.

Nowadays a man literally masturbates himself with the woman, and he thinks that is love. He makes the movements up and down as he is masturbating himself; his thought is in his own sexual fantasies instead in his own presence in love. He is having sex with a magazine woman or movie or past relations, not with the woman he loves; that is why he feels that sex is an aggression. Nobody has told him how to do it, and he learns only through pornography.

The movement up and down does not exist in nature, unless there is an earthquake. Animals do that because they are following an instinct of procreation, but the true man in his divine form does not do that; his movements are left to right in a gentle manner, while she is holding the phallus in her womb, embracing love.

131

Watch nature, how she moves and how the sun caresses her in a gentle manner.

A man who ejaculates is very aggressive and destructive in his behavior because of his lack of connection. Celibacy is another form of rejection of the feminine, the Holy Spirit.

There is a powerful and sad story of this monk. He was praying and praying, then he saw this beautiful light all around, and he had an erection. With all these teachings about sex being bad, he felt so guilty that he begin to punish himself and end in suicide.

In ancient times, celibacy was a path of enlightenment. There is a lot of energy that gets blocked or lost with this encounter, with the misunderstanding of sacred sex, so the saints preferred not to have sex to make their path easier, so they didn't have a wife or husband to deal with. Yet, repression of the sex will create a distortion in the self because there is the fear of love.

Premature ejaculation impedes the man to open the door for the altar in a woman. It is, indeed, a form of impotence.

He relates his manhood only through the penis, he truly thinks that is where the manhood resides; he forgot that the manhood is not a part of his body, but a divine position in the universe, and the manhood is in many realms of the self. He must conquer himself through will power to achieve his own enlightenment. As much he wants to control others he will loose his own will power, and be controlled by what he wants to control so badly.

A woman feels abandoned in her inner core when a man prematurely ejaculates or when he cannot have an erection. She feels the lack of love and rejection and she will lose the passion of love, and eventually she will blame herself, again, for not being enough women as the system taught her. She will be unbalanced in all her chakras, and her dark side will grow. A woman will feel guilty because of her fragile understanding about sex; she buys the idea that she is responsible for his impotence or sex problems. He usually blames her too, to cover his own guiltiness, and she believes. There are many women who do not have an orgasm because of this reason, she feels that she is there to please him, whenever he wants to, so she is there holding her pain without understanding sex and thinking that she will lose him if she does not agree with him because he has been manipulating her to cover his own guiltiness.

Woman truly thinks that she needs to do whatever it takes to keep him happy; that it is her responsibility as a woman to give him pleasure and will accept anything that he asks her to do. Is that love? Nobody was there to teach her or him...

Woman is the teacher of love, a teacher who didn't know that she was teaching. She was teaching love in the silence, in acceptance, in the shame, in her pain. Now the ways of the woman's teachings are to explain to the man what making love means and how she feels, yet, she is not there anymore to "regenerate the man". She has been doing this for centuries, and it didn't work; she is there to be a woman, and by doing this, the teacher is there for the man, not for the spoiled boy who only wants to masturbate himself.

Nowadays, this understanding is lost, and most people use sex for degeneration of the true self of human beings. When sex is performed with ego involved, the portal is opened, but it is open to many dark beings that will create hurt in the heart of humans

135

and the fear of love.

When sex is done in lower chakras only, the relationship splits eventually because it creates separation; everything is interconnected, you will experience things that do not belong to you, nasty spirits that will control you from your lower chakras, then a lower vibration will be there until you clean all that mess that impedes spiritual growth. That situation will be there for long time.

In the ancient times, the woman is prepared for long time, since childhood, we used to make sacred dance part of the training for sacred sex; sacred dance is not a belly dancing, but a dance that you encounter in yourself.

Sacred dance is a path of a woman to find her divinity; she will dance her spirit in all the ways that are possible, she will encounter her fears and joys, her wounds and her love, she will heal herself through the dance, she finds her past, present and future and moves herself through the universe. When a woman "finds her dance" the universe rejoices!

Sacred dance was one of the practices that were done at the temple; men were not allowed in those dances, for it was a sacred place for the woman.

The dance of the seven veils is a sacred dance, only to be performed for a man who is in a woman's trust one hundred percent, a man who she is willing to give her light, a man who understands what a woman is.

Magdala made the dance of the seven veils with the Christ as part of the ceremony; she removed the seven veils, not precisely the seven demons, as is manipulated.

Here is a description of the seven veils dance.

The Seven Veils

....The pure love is the one who came from the soul, doesn't have bottom or top,...behind ..front...

It is the pure sensation, the total surrender of the self..

The love satisfies itself, without touching the selfish points...

Love is liberator by essence, comprehensive and compassionate, constructor and destructor...

Love can never be measured; it is found in the fountain of the endless self, the waters that never end...

Love never begins or ends, love just is, because it is the essence of the soul , the God within......

Love is the connection with the divine within, always present, surrendered, free, calm, loyal witness
To express that pure love the veils must be withdrawn like the sacred dance, the Sacred Dance of endless love...
The dance to understand love has begun since the beginning of always.......
The first veil to be removed is the one who holds the hair, this veil is tangled in the hair, and in order to removed the intention must be created, until our hair runs free like the Wind, with this the surrender of pride and judgment,, and the freedom that provokes takes us beyond the limitation of the thinking process,...
As we let go this veil and enjoy the freedom with our hair so wild... we realize about the next veil, the veil that covers the eyes, it is very beautiful purple, the blindness, the no direction! that is pain in action! Yes , we can see! when we decide to remove it, truth is found, finally we find our direction and the

ultimate beauty   is discovered, truth is in
front of us, we see the majestic of the great
mother, the stars and moon! the deep and
clarity of the children's eyes, nothing is
hidden anymore , pain is gone, and freedom
is found because of truth! It is not an image
anymore it is the realization of the self!.......
But still many veils to be withdrawn!
We can see the veil that covers our mouth
and throat; it is blue like the sky! so
beautiful! and light! it most go too! it is the
same mouth that we kiss and bless, but also
it is the shout from within that we never did,
there are so many silences and anguishes
being held in that veil! Yes truth must be
shouted, and at the time of that surrender, a
song of freedom comes out from the soul!...
Slowly, and almost shyly, we realize the veil
that is holding our heart; it is green, as the
forest! It is tightly, suppressing, covering the
heart, there is so much pain to let go! So
afraid to be hurt! so we dance by whirling
and whirling and the veil gets loosen, as if it

has no reason to be there, covering our
breast, now in freedom to nourish the self
and every soul, and the sensation of pure
love begins the dance!, finally we find the
love for own selves, the fountain of the
endless love.... in this surrender the com
passion is discovered,, to the own self and
every soul that is around us! We are never
going to be hurt again ...love provides by
itself!
In this beautiful Sacred dance of the
freedom the veil that is holding our waist, is
remove, like a consequence, like life by
itself, destiny, yellow is the color, and with
this we surrender the will to the eternal
femininity within, to the one who knows, this
part of the self that has the knowledge of
everything, the whole history is in her skin!
It is the teacher, sister, mother, daughter; it
is the woman, the transformer,
....   The light Giver!
The wanting to control and have power
over others is gone! And with that our

slavery is over....
But we still see the orange veil! With this we
see the desire, another pain to be removed,
another veil to be removed it gets tangled
around the legs, falling so slowly! And when
it touches the ground the understanding of
duality finds the way to unity! A new
liberation in taking place! But it is one
more, still, one veil to be removed the red of
life! It is the connection with life, the fear is
there in it, and we must die to live! says this
voice inside the self!, we are afraid to be so
naked! But finally in the passion of the
dance that veil is gone!
And with that comes the understanding of
the eternal life!
The whole being is integrated,
it vibrates as whole!,
sensation of the manifestation
of life love and light is surrounding the
being,
in a continuum dance of the sacredness of
the self!, In the nakedness of this surrender

*we show ourselves the crystal within it is the
love of the Christ inside that shines all over
the self, finally nothing to hide, there is no
more pain, no time or timeless, no more
limitations, chains are broken in the eternal
surrender of love!*

Magdala

*Nowadays, there is no school for a
woman, but we will create a school again.
At the ceremony of love, she gets prepared
for light, meaning that she finds a higher
state of consciousness. She prays and stays
connected to the spirit. She dresses herself
and creates the temple, a sacred place in a
beautiful manner. She cleans herself in
body, mind and spirit; she is prepared to
receive the prayer. She knows deep inside*

that she will share part of her mystery and that is a special event to her. She will tremble as the waters that come out from her womb connect with the whole universe.

Love will make her wet and that holy water will purify her; she is indeed getting clean for the surrender to the spirit.

Love is always the way. She will know that a beautiful journey is just about to begin. She is the door and the key and the willingness of the spirit for unity through love.

When a marriage was going to take place, all the women gathered together to prepare the bride for sacred sex; they used to bath her with roses and sing to her, and the wise woman came to guide her in the womanhood.

In many tribes, this ceremony took place,

*it was a beautiful ceremony, a woman grew
up understanding and embracing the
womanhood since she had the first moon
time. She was blessed by all women.*

*Nowadays, that ceremony has been
translated in something completely
nonsense, the "showers" , as we know them
are a version of that original ceremony, but
women have forgotten the purpose of the
ceremony; there are no more wise women to
guide a woman, nobody speaks anymore
about sacred sex and the beauty of it and the
work that we have as a woman.*

*The lack of knowledge of sex in the
system has brought the woman to think that
orgasm is about the clitoris, and when that
happens she immediately begins to get dry.
She will not allow the sacred phallus in her
anymore, and she will reject the ceremony,
refusing to trust him and not share her light
with him, and eventually, she will began to*

145

*see sex as something that is a "duty"
because she is "married", as the system put
on her, so she won't be present anymore at
the ceremony; she will begin to distance
herself from her lover, and sometimes to find
another lover to make her feel the illusion of
love. She has forgotten that she is, indeed,
the Great Mother's daughter, and she has
forgotten her sacredness.*

*Woman needs to trust him and feel the
appreciation that he has for her; she needs
to embrace her own sacredness and uncover
her temple inside. She needs to trust who she
is. In other words, she has forgotten her own
male side that she needs to trust.*

*Woman needs to feel secure and safe
with the man she loves in order to open
herself, to open the altar within her.*

When she has an orgasm by the womb,

*an endless energy so powerful will uncover
and connect all the worlds of light where
human beings really belong. The power of
the orgasm from the womb of light is far
beyond any description or technique that
people want to follow.*

*Orgasm in the womb will bring the water
that never ends; she will never be dry and
can be connected for a very long time.*

*Sexual energy is drawn upward because
of love, in the ways of the Great Mother
love. The awakening of divine compassion
takes place; it is the new beginning, the new
understanding, and the higher vibration to
reach new worlds inside. Enlightenment
takes place.*

*Be very selective with whom you are
going to perform the sacred love ceremony;
pray and pray to allow the spirit to choose.,
be prepared, find your male within yourself,*

stay connected in the light. From this will
depend your own spirit, your family, your
community, and your enlightenment.

 As Moses lifted up the serpent in the
wilderness, even so must the Son of man be
lifted up; that whosoever believeth on him
should not perish, but have everlasting life.

 — *John 3:14, 15*

Kundalini

Kundalini is the creative life force that all human beings have since they were born; it is the root of the tree that must journey into the 33 vertebrae all the way to the top for the Enlightenment.

It is represented by the snake that is asleep and must be awakened. Through love in sacred sex, the serpent awakens and as she goes upwards, the consciousness goes inward, and becomes the true refection of Father-Mother in perfect balance and unity; it is a divine bliss.

Kundalini is a knowledge that has been in this planet in many tribes, for Aztec and Mayan it is represented by Quetzatcoatl, the feathered serpent.

Quetzatcoatl

Ascension means to go up, it means to align all the chakras in complete harmony with the all, the perfect and natural way for human beings, male and female forces, to join together, heart and mind, joined together.

It is truly unnatural to think that feminine energy is a dark force, when she is, indeed, the Holy Spirit.

Serpent Mound In Ohio, is a beautiful representation of this knowledge.

Questions from the Sisterhood

Please describe the role of the man in marriage (and the woman).

Man is a protector in the outside, the woman is a protector in the inside; the man will protect life, even with his own life, he is there for the protection of the woman and children, he is indeed the one who follows the law of divine order, and he does this through love and because of love, but he does not impose harmony; he simply follows the ways of love. For the man, his wife is his home.

Woman will protect the man and her children; she will take care of him in the most loving way. Taking care of him means providing him with light in his path, she will co- create a beautiful world with him

153

because of love, she will hold unity and wisdom. She will look for the highest good of the family; she is home and she will keep it sacred, she will stay connected to the spirit to do this, she will create the space for growth in the family and use her love and powers to embrace harmony.

He-she will be as one, for he is the true image of her male side, and she is he true image of his feminine side; both are the perfect harmony, there is nothing to hide; the nakedness of the heart remains intact.

He is in charge of the manifestation that she, the heart, creates for the highest good of all.

How will Sacred Sex affect my marriage?

Your marriage will be a true marriage in the long run; removing the guiltiness and the blockage of sex will create a beautiful, powerful relationship between man and woman and create with this a beautiful family, then community, then country, world, and it all starts in your bed.

Yet in the beginning, there will be much struggle, the men are not ready for this knowledge; he will feel challenged and destructive, like a boy without his candy. This knowledge will bring war instead of peace, until he begins to grow within himself; he is used to taking the power of the feminine; if the feminine does not give him the power he will shout and be angry about it, and sacred sex is not about giving the power away, but to consummate him in his divine nature.

We are giving birth to the new world; we do want the men, the manifestation, there, but with honor and respect for life. Honor and respect is a beautiful way to express love.

Sacred dance, sacred sex, how does the modern woman go back to embrace the teachings of sacred sex? How do we start?

Woman is the teacher of love; what do you want to teach? You will start by embracing your own light, your sacredness within. This means that everything that you do is sacred; in the ordinary is where the extraordinary takes place. Change the image that you have about yourself, change it for the true woman that you are, a daughter of the Great Mother.

Woman starts by focusing in the light; this means that the thought of guiltiness and separation will go away with the energy of love; that is where your light resides. You want love, and then create love within the self.

As you do this, you will manifest love in your life; it is the new vibration within yourself, and people around you, relationships, will move through this new vibration, for you are embracing a beautiful you.

Find your dance within yourself, see in every woman your sister, and stay focused in that light.

Then, from that light you will ask for more light, and understanding will grow within you, and new doors will be discovered within yourself. You are enlightening your consciousness and making the outside the expression of love, the same as the inside, your true love, the holy water that never ends, the essence of all life, the light that you are.

Remember that love is the most powerful energy because it comes directly from the divine, and it is in your heart. Only true human beings are able to love, yet love has no gender, it is pure in the essence, in the heart, then it is expressed in many ways, all the spectrum of colors, yet you do want to express the love in the purest form, it is beyond tradition or cultural belief or color of the skin.

Love is the bonding of all, the unity, the oneness.

Sacred sex feels so abstract, and we women

158

*have forgotten the language of the abstract
and want the things in a concrete manner.
Hhow we can embrace that abstract world
that we have forgotten?*

*Sacred sex has been exposed as a
technique, positions, People wanted a
tradition, a way to start with number one
and continue, but it didn't work either,
because the feminine, the abstract world
was missing.*

*Woman will remember the language of
the abstract when she begins to make her
spiritual work and listens to the voice
within, and discerns that voice from many
voices within. She will decode the messages
from the spirit as she grows within the self.
She will begin to trust herself a hundred
percent; she will begin to be-live; believing
in herself means that she will be present
within the self. Then the abstract language*

*will unfold, when she begins to embrace her
own femininity; honor her within you.*

Can you give us techniques anyway?

*The problem with techniques is that some
work for one person and they might not
work for some others, I truly recommend
that you create your own technique; your
own way will be unfolded as you grow
within the self.*

*As I have been saying, there were many
initiations in the ancient temples for woman
and for men. Now what we are doing? How
will we start our work? You ask.*

Start by valuing yourself, finding the value

that you truly have, start by being selective
about the men in your life and the kind of
sex that you are having, question your
images about sex.

Meditate, write your troubles and then
burn them with sage and cedar and copal,
pray, go to sweat lodge, go to spiritual
feminine school, dance, look how you are
feeding yourself, I am talking about spiritual
food, what are you reading? Seeing beauty?
Have an encounter with yourself, go to
vision quest for women. Listen to the Great
Mother within you, have a journal, sing.

Eat beauty, listen to the voice of the
Great Mother, she is not a bully nor angry;
her voice is very similar to your voice, she
always leaves a door open for you to keep
on asking, just sit and ask her questions and
have a paper in front of you and just write
down what you hear; you will be surprised
of your own wisdom!

Sing, sing your songs, for her and for you, just let them come out from your heart.

Love and be focused in how you are loving, and that will take you to your inside world, the masculine way, or go to your inside world and feel the love in all your cells, all your atoms, and then let it out in such an incredible energy, the feminine ways, practice both.

Watch the stars and hear the beautiful orchestra, walk in nature and listen to the beautiful orchestra.

Be present, means, as you speak, listen to everything around you, feel all your body and the vibration, and your voice at the same time, and observe yourself. Magical things will happen.

There are also many meditations that you

can use, rainbow meditation for the chakras is my favorite, and you will raise your kundalini and enter in a beautiful world within you.

Look at yourself in the mirror, do not think of anything, you do that by observing your own breath and focus in your third eye at the same time, you will be surprised what you can find.

Find friends who are also in the spiritual work, watch your speech, how much energy you throw away when you speak third dimensionally. Energy is so precious, you need all the power within yourself to transmute yourself, and you need to transmute yourself before trying to transmute others, Observe your own presence all the time. Witness yourself.

Presence means that you are being aware of yourself, all yourself, using your senses,

your medicine; when I said bring the
presence of your own presence is to bring
the witness of all your being.

Conclusion

The planet is changing, and human beings must change with her, she is indeed, doing a new dance, a dance that is creating a new way to perceive reality, a new way to relate to each other and within the self.

The emerging of the feminine is taking place all over the world; the women are receiving the call from the Great Mother, to return back to the sacredness of the feminine. It is, indeed, the time of the women to embrace her as a sacred being. Yet there is so much to embrace, to understand, to uncover, to connect and disconnect, to let go and dance in the new path of the sacredness of life. And we are just in time; the door is open for all life forms to embrace their divinity.

Sex has been an issue for so long; it has been a blockage for the people, because of the lack of understanding of sex. Sex is the door where human beings came to this realm, the place of the duality, and the way to move on is to become One, again, within the self.
The new born being will bring the energy where the conception took place.

This is not a feminist book, but an ancient knowledge of womanhood, women need to make their work; the women are the saviors of the world, and we must clean ourselves from wrong beliefs and make our work as women.

This knowledge is for the sacredness of life, in all the forms that life can be expressed. We as women are creating a new reality, a new way with the recognition of the freedom of the spirit as our right as a human being.

Love is the bonding of all tribes, inside the self and manifested outside the self, in the whole world, so finally peace and harmony can be uncovered as a natural way of living. It is, indeed, through the integration of the self what will bring peace into the world.

Human beings have grown enough now that they ready to embrace this knowledge.

This ancient knowledge is not about the destruction of the male ways, but indeed, is to consummate them in their own ways, because they represent the manifestation of reality. We, as women, have the power to transmute and change the manifestation. We do this in our ordinary ways, where the extraordinary takes place, with our work and our presence.

This knowledge will create in the beginning a commotion in the relationships, already pre-established, all the changes bring commotion, yet they will bring unity through love and understanding into the families.

I am truly waiting for your return call for we are dancing back into the Great Mother's way, all together.

I am your other you

Magdala

Appendix

Ana Kingsford in 1880 found this ancient writing...

**A Prophecy of the Kingdom of the Soul,
mystically called the Day of the Woman[1]**

1. And now I show you a mystery and a new thing, which is part of the mystery of the fourth day of creation.

2. The word which shall come to save the world, shall be uttered by a woman.

3. A woman shall conceive, and shall bring forth the tidings of salvation.

4. For the reign of Adam is at its last hour; and God shall crown all things by the creation of Eve.

5. Hitherto the man hath been alone, and hath had dominion over the earth.

6. But when the woman shall be created, God shall give unto her the kingdom; and she shall be first in rule and highest in dignity.

7. Yea, the last shall be first; and the elder shall serve the younger.

8. So that women shall no more lament for their womanhood: but men shall rather say, "O that we had been born women!"

9. For the strong shall be put down from their seat; and the meek shall be exalted to their place.

10. The days of the covenant of manifestation are passing away: the gospel of interpretation cometh.

11. There shall nothing new be told; but that which is ancient shall be interpreted.

12. So that man the manifestor shall resign his office; and woman the interpreter shall give light to the world.

13. Hers is the fourth office: she revealeth that which the Lord hath manifested.

14. Hers is the light of the heavens, and the brightest of the planets of the holy seven.

15. She is the fourth dimension; the eyes which enlighten; the power which draweth inward to God.

16. And her kingdom cometh; the day of the exaltation of woman.

17. And her reign shall be greater than the reign of the man; for Adam shall be put down from his place; and she shall have dominion for ever.

18. And she who is alone shall bring forth more children to God than she who hath an husband.

19. There shall no more be a reproach against women: but against men shall be the reproach.

20. For the woman is the crown of man, and the final manifestation of humanity.

21. She is the nearest to the throne of God, when she shall be revealed.

22. But the creation of woman is not yet complete: but it shall be complete in the time which is at hand.

23. All things are thine, O Mother of God: all things are thine, O Thou who risest from the sea; and Thou shalt have dominion over all the worlds.

1. Paris, February 7, 1880. See note to Part 1. This Illumination refers not to persons, but to principles--*e.g.* the "man" and "woman" of the mind are the intellect and intuition, respectively; and, while "Adam" is the old Adam of sense, "Eve" is the soul.   S. H. H.

Solomon writings...

The excellence of wisdom: how she is to be found.

1 I myself also am a mortal man, like all others, and of the race of him, that was first made of the earth, and in the womb of my mother I was fashioned to be flesh.

2 In the time of ten months I was compacted in blood, of the seed of man, and the pleasure of sleep concurring.

3 And being born I drew in the common air, and fell upon the earth, that is made alike, and the first voice which I uttered was crying, as all others do.

4 I was nursed in swaddling clothes, and with great cares.

5 For none of the kings had any other beginning of birth.

6 For all men have one entrance into life, and the like going out.

7 Wherefore I wished, and understanding was given me: and I called upon God, and the spirit of wisdom came upon me:

8 And I preferred her before kingdoms and thrones, and esteemed riches nothing in comparison of her.

9 Neither did I compare unto her any precious stone: for all gold in comparison of her, is as a little sand, and silver in respect to her shall be counted as clay.

10 I loved her above health and beauty, and chose to have her instead of light: for her light cannot be put out.

11 Now all good things came to me together with her, and innumerable riches through her hands,

12 And I rejoiced in all these: for this wisdom went before me, and I knew not that she was the mother of them all.

13 Which I have learned without guile, and communicate without envy, and her riches I hide not.

14 For she is an infinite treasure to men! which they that use, become the friends of God, being commended for the gift of discipline.

15 And God hath given to me to speak as I would, and to conceive thoughts worthy of

those things that are given me: because he is the guide of wisdom, and the director of the wise:

16 For in his hand are both we, and our words, and all wisdom, and the knowledge and skill of works.

17 For he hath given me the true knowledge of the things that are: to know the disposition of the whole world, and the virtues of the elements,

18 The beginning, and ending, and midst of the times, the alterations of their courses, and the changes of seasons,

19 The revolutions of the year, and the dispositions of the stars,

20 The natures of living creatures, and rage of wild beasts, the force of winds, and

reasonings of men, the diversities of plants, and the virtues of roots,

21 And all such things as are hid and not foreseen, I have learned: for wisdom, which is the worker of all things, taught me.

22 For in her is the spirit of understanding: holy, one, manifold, subtile, eloquent, active, undefiled, sure, sweet, loving that which is good, quick, which nothing hindereth, beneficent,

23 Gentle, kind, steadfast, assured, secure, having all power, overseeing all things, and containing all spirits, intelligible, pure, subtile.

24 For wisdom is more active than all active things: and reacheth everywhere by reason of her purity.

25 For she is a vapor of the power of God, and a certain pure emanation of the glory of the almighty God: and therefore no defiled thing cometh into her.

26 For she is the brightness of eternal light, and the unspotted mirror of God's majesty, and the image of his goodness.

27 And being but one, she can do all things: and remaining in herself the same, she reneweth all things, and through nations conveyeth herself into holy souls, she maketh the friends of God and prophets.

28 For God loveth none but him that dwelleth with wisdom.

29 For she is more beautiful than the sun, and above all the order of the stars: being compared with the light, she is found before it.

30 For after this cometh night, but no evil can overcome wisdom.

Further praises of wisdom: and her fruits.

1 She reacheth therefore from end to end mightily, and ordereth all things sweetly.

2 Her have I loved, and have sought her out from my youth, and have desired to take her for my spouse, and I became a lover of her beauty.

3 She glorifieth her nobility by being conversant with God: yea and the Lord of all things hath loved her.

4 For it is she that teacheth the knowledge of God, and is the chooser of his works.

5 And if riches be desired in life, what is richer than wisdom, which maketh all things?

6 And if sense do work: who is a more artful worker than she of those things that are?

7 And if a man love justice: her labors have great virtues; for she teacheth temperance, and prudence, and justice, and fortitude, which are such things as men can have nothing more profitable in life.

8 And if a man desire much knowledge: she knoweth things past, and judgeth of things to come: she knoweth the subtilties of speeches, and the solutions of arguments: she knoweth signs and wonders before they be done, and the events of times and ages.

9 I purposed therefore to take her to me to live with me: knowing that she will

communicate to me of her good things, and will be a comfort in my cares and grief.

10 For her sake I shall have glory among the multitude, and honour with the ancients, though I be young:

11 And I shall be found of a quick conceit in judgment, and shall be admired in the sight of the mighty, and the faces of princes shall wonder at me.

12 They shall wait for me when I hold my peace, and they shall look upon me when I speak, and if I talk much they shall lay their hands on their mouths.

13 Moreover by the means of her I shall have immortality: and shall leave behind me an everlasting memory to them that come after me.

14 I shall set the people in order: and nations shall be subject to me.

15 Terrible kings hearing shall be afraid of me: among the multitude I shall be found good, and valiant in war.

16 When I go into my house, I shall repose myself with her: for her conversation hath no bitterness, nor her company any tediousness, but joy and gladness.

17 Thinking these things with myself, and pondering them in my heart, that to be allied to wisdom is immortality,

18 And that there is great delight in her friendship, and inexhaustible riches in the works of her hands, and in the exercise of conference with her, wisdom, and glory in the communication of her words: I went about seeking, that I might take her to myself.

19 And I was a witty child and had received a good soul.

20 And whereas I was more good, I came to a body undefiled.

From the Secret book of Thomas

This is the first power which was before all of them (and) which came forth from his mind, She is the forethought of the All - her light shines like his light - the perfect power which is the image of the invisible, virginal Spirit who is perfect. The first power, the glory of Barbelo, the perfect glory in the aeons, the glory of the revelation, she glorified the virginal Spirit and it was she

who praised him, because thanks to him she
had come forth. This is the first thought, his
image; she became the womb of everything,
for it is she who is prior to them all, the
Mother-Father, the first man, the holy Spirit,
the thrice-male, the thrice-powerful, the
thrice-named androgynous one, and the
eternal aeon among the invisible ones, and
the first to come forth.

About the Author

Magdala Ramirez is a Medicine Women who was born in Mexico and lived among the pyramids and ancient wisdom of the Maya and Aztec people. Now she is living in a place called "the place where the waters comes out from the womb" in the forest of Arkansas. She was trained in her work from a very early age, spending many years studying and sharing information with the elders of knowledge near her home. She has worked 35 years with the knowledge of the feminine ways, warrior women and sacred dance. Ramirez has conducted workshops and lectures in Mexico and the Untied States, and is the Author of "The Union of Polarities", "I Am You" both books are Available on Amazon.com

She also wrote the "Mayan Runes" available at mariomagdala@yahoo.com

For Seminars, comments and books information, write to Magdala at Po Box. Harrison AR 72602
Or email at mariomagdala@yahoo.com.